An Inuk Boy Becomes A Hunter

Map of the
homeland of John Igloliorte

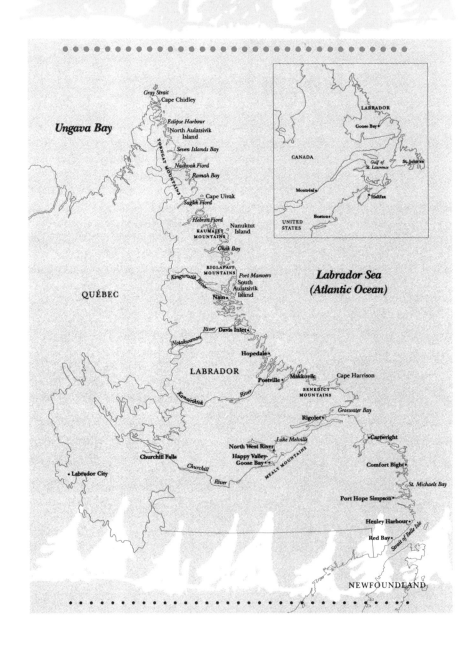

An Inuk Boy Becomes A Hunter

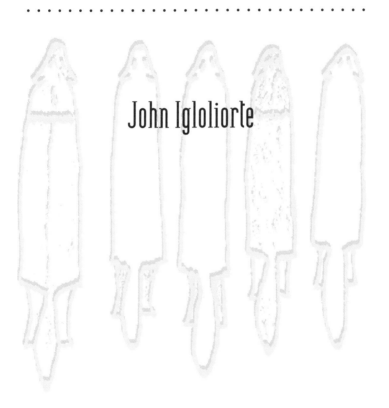

John Igloliorte

NIMBUS
PUBLISHING

Nimbus Publishing Limited
PO Box 9166
Halifax, NS B3K 5M8
(902) 455-4286

Drawings: John Igloliorte
Design: Kathy Kaulbach, Halifax
Printed and bound in Canada by Transcontinental

Canadian Cataloguing in Publication Data
Igloliorte, John.
An Inuk boy becomes a hunter
ISBN 1-55109-051-1

1. Igloliorte, John. 2. Inuit youth – Newfoundland – Labrador – Biography. 3. Inuit youth – Newfoundland – Labrador – Social life and customs. 4. Labrador (Nfld.) – Biography. 5. Labrador (Nfld.) – Social life and customs. I. Title.
E99.E7I44 1994   971.8'2004971   C94-950140-9

This book is dedicated
to all our native peoples
who have lived the
struggle of change.

Contents

Introduction

John Igloliorte was born into a rich heritage that is as much the story of Labrador as the harsh and beautiful landscape of the region he still calls home.

For hundreds of years, Inuit of northern Labrador employed their ingenuity, courage, and deep sense of community in an ongoing battle to survive the elements. In the process, they developed a spirituality that had to be strong enough to endure the challenges of their environment. This powerful inner life, as much as their many skills, enabled them to endure a rigorous way of life, travelling by dogsled along the coast and through the barren-lands and forests for weeks at a time to hunt the caribou and seals that would sustain them through a long winter, providing both food and most of their bedding and clothing as well.

Growing up in the village of Nain in the 1940s and '50s plunged Igloliorte into the rigours of a demanding life, in which a boy became a man at thirteen. He faced new challenges, too: the presence of an economy based not on cooperation for the purpose of survival but on money meant that

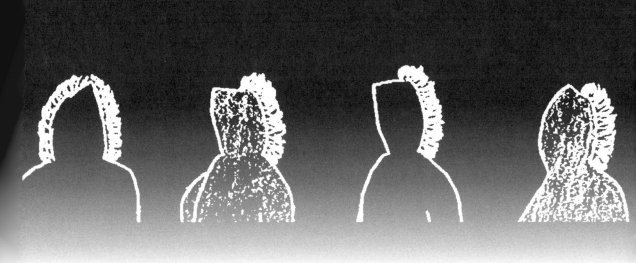

Inuit hunters like Igloliorte were compelled to search for ways to turn their skills to financial purposes. The cod and the seals, along with the firewood they cut all year, provided only a marginal living.

Yet Igloliorte, like the community he describes, also experienced times of great happiness. A balmy spring day after a long winter was cause enough for the whole village to turn out for a picnic, and festivities throughout the year celebrated each resident's contributions to the community. And the very hardships that were part of a hunter's life brought with them another kind of joy—the joy of learning skills and gaining knowledge that had been passed down through generations.

In these words and drawings, Igloliorte provides us with a pathway into a way of life that is fast disappearing, and with it a hope that cries out to be rekindled.

Gary Baikie
Director, Torngasok Cultural Centre
Nain, Labrador

Our Ancestors Told Stories

I am fascinated by this rock in the shape of a polar bear, so I am drawing it. The rock looks just like a polar bear from the distance. It's a big rock with a slight crack in it.

When I went to look at it up close, I couldn't see the bear in the rock right away. It doesn't look anything like a polar bear when you see it up close.

I was told by the old men in Nain that it once *was* a polar bear.

There is also a big dog that you can see in the rock face. The dog is facing the polar bear. According to legend, this dog barked at the polar bear. The polar bear was said to be attacking by surprise.

I didn't see the polar bear and the dog turn to rock; I have only heard the story. The story says that the polar bear was about to destroy the people of Nain when a shaman petrified it.

Before we became Christians, it is said that Inuit shamans used to exert all kinds of power. That was eons ago, long before I was ever born, for sure.

Those are the kinds of stories that the old men used to tell. They would tell stories about all kinds of frightening things, superstitions or hallucinations. Our ancestors were always telling stories.

When Memory Begins

My earliest memories begin at the age of five.

I was born in 1936 in Nain, which is on the north-
east coast of Labrador. That's where I live today.

We used to live in a long, rectangular house—my
grandfather, my uncle, my parents, and myself. My father
could not walk and rarely left the bed. He had tuberculosis.
But he used to play the organ in church, and some men used
to come and haul him to church so he could play. Even in
summer he couldn't walk, because he was paralyzed somehow
from the tuberculosis.

My family was the poorest in the village. We were so poor
that sometimes I had to go to the minister's house to ask for a
bowl of soup for my father. But I usually wasn't conscious of
our poverty. Most of my thoughts were of playing.

We children would play anywhere at all. I particularly
remember an old rock along the shore, which we would pre-
tend was an island and from which we killed many make-
believe monsters. Discarded dishes and such we would use as
play dishes. Even though we were aware of being boys, we
didn't mind playing with dishes, because there weren't too
many other toys for us to play with.

Come spring, we'd make bows and arrows out of old
wooden barrels, willows, and twigs. We searched everywhere
for empty cartridges to place at the tips of the arrows. These
things we used as ways of learning how to hunt animals. With

our bows and arrows, we would kill snow-
birds for food. And sometimes we would just kill
them with rocks.

I remember killing my first bird. It had a broken
wing, and I chased it for a long time. Whenever I got close
to it, I tried to fall on it with my whole body, but it kept es-
caping. It was still alive when I finally caught it, so I chopped
its head off to make sure it was dead.

Then I went into the house to show my father my first
kill. He put it in a safe place until I could give it to my god-
mother. When she saw it, she bit me on my hands so that I
would grow up to be a good hunter. That was a custom we
knew as children.

We had other ways of learning to hunt, some of which we
invented ourselves—like using snowshoes to trap birds, catching them in the mesh. None of the grownups objected to what
we were doing, because they knew we were just trying to learn
the skills we would need later.

When spring waned, to be replaced by summer, we put
away our bows and arrows and began fashioning slingshots
out of sealskin. They were two-and-a-half feet long and could
shoot rocks really far. We used them to kill beach-birds, but
sometimes, just as we did when we used bows and arrows, we
put the slingshots down and just used the rocks to kill birds.

On the Beach

One day, after spring break-up, a ship arrived. It belonged to MacMillan, a rich American who sailed in his schooner up the coast of Labrador every year—not to hunt, just to see the sights. In those days, the Inuit brass band would go out in their motorboats to meet ships, blowing their trumpets to welcome anybody who was coming into the harbour, whether it was MacMillan or the crew of one of the supply boats bringing fruit, vegetables, wood, fishing tackle, or other goods into Nain. Being a small boy, I always followed the people who went out to meet the boats.

That particular day, we brought MacMillan ashore with us and watched him closely as he gingerly walked along the edge of the boat towards the ladder on the wharf. But before he got to the ladder, he suddenly fell into the water. I tried not to laugh, but when I heard someone else start up, my laughter just burst out of me. What a good laugh I had! And when he popped out from under the water, with his eyeglasses on and all, I laughed all the harder. As for MacMillan, he had to return to his boat to change before he could come ashore.

We children were always happy when ships came to Nain, because we would be offered candies by the crew when they stopped to buy second-hand guns for their hunting trips up north. We hardly ever got candy otherwise.

But even without candy, we always had a good time when summer came. One thing we liked to do was chase small trout down by the shore or along the brooks, catching them by hitting them with pieces of barrel hoops. There were always pieces of old barrels around that had been used to hold salted cod until the wood was no good any more. When we began chasing trout along the beach, we'd take off our boots and place them on top of a big rock. But sometimes we'd forget about them, and the rising tide would wash them away. That meant having to go home barefoot, and in great fear of being bawled out.

It wasn't just because of the boots that I was afraid, though. I knew I wasn't supposed to be on the beach, because my mother said the tides were too dangerous. I always promised not to go, but as soon as my buddies came along, I'd be headed right back to the beach with them again.

One day when we were swimming, someone said, "Your mother is coming!" When I heard that, I just scooted all the way home, leaving my clothes behind on the beach.

My father was certainly surprised when I ran into the house bare-naked! Since he couldn't move, I just jumped under the blankets next to him, figuring this was a pretty good place to hide. He didn't say anything to give me away, but my mother found me anyway, grabbed me by the arm, and spanked me on the behind. You should have heard me crying!

Later that summer, my mother went out one day, and my father stayed home in bed, as usual. I didn't go out to the beach, but sat looking through the window, watching two men who had gone out to anchor a motorboat. One of them was in the motorboat, and the other was in a "flat," dragging the anchor into place.

Suddenly the man in the flat fell into the water, and by the time the other guy got him out, he looked as stiff as a board. I thought he was dead, for sure. But he finally started to move again, and after a short time they both came ashore.

My father could tell just by looking at me that something was wrong, and asked what I was looking at. "Nothing," I told him. That was all I said. I told him that lie because I didn't want my mother to think I had been playing on the beach and had seen the accident. But I'm not sure if he believed me.

Changes

Other than those few stories, I can't remember that much about my father, because he passed away when I was very little. I don't even know how old I was when he died. The only part I remember is my mother leading me by the hand in the graveyard and telling me that my father had gone to see Lord Jesus.

I don't know how long I stayed with my mother after that. But I do know that I was fostered for a while by a man named John Flagg—myself and another Inuk child, Elizabeth Green. Fostering is like adoption. It just means living with another family if your family can't provide for you.

John Flagg lived in Nain, but sometimes he took us camping at a place called Paul's Island, and when we came back from camping, we would stay either with him or with another family if he was going to be away for a long time. Then, when I was a little older, I was fostered by another man, Titus Joshua, and sometimes I would stay with other people, too. But this would be during the holidays. The rest of the year I lived in the mission school in Nain and saw my mother, my other relatives, or my foster family on Sunday. Sometimes they came to church with us kids from the school, and after church we would all have dinner together. We would spend some of the festive days together, too—especially Christmas.

I used to be really shy of all these people who looked after me, and I could hardly look into their eyes. I missed my own family a lot. But I did get to see my mother fairly often. And I went back to live with her when I left school. That was when I was thirteen.

An Inuk boy becomes a man at thirteen.
At least, that's the way it was back then.

The Mission School

When I was first in school, we kids used to see a lot of planes flying north. One time I counted seventeen planes flying in formation. It turned out there was a war on, World War II, but to the people in Nain, the war seemed very far away—except for all the planes, and except when it was over. When the people heard the war was over, they began shooting their guns in celebration. Then, right in front of my eyes, they started filling a chunk of wood with black powder—a home-made cannon. It exploded and dis-appeared into thin air! That was the first time I had ever seen explosives. Another bomb I saw that was made by Inuit used iron and a pipe. I was amazed when the explosion tore apart the iron.

But I didn't spend all my time counting planes and watching bombs go off. I had to go to school, starting every September. Our school was attended by students from all over Labrador, maybe about fifty children in four different classes.

We all lived in the school, too, in two separate buildings—one for the girls, one for the boys. My bed was up in the attic of the main school building; the other kids and I slept on the floor, on long mattresses placed side by side.

The school and the manse had lights from a small generator, which would be shut off at 11:00 P.M., and we Inuit kids also used kerosene lamps. Be-ing kids, of course, we did make quite a lot of noise up there at night, and sometimes our teacher would get quite frustrated by it. So we might have to go to bed early the next night, right after supper, at about seven o'clock; this also happened if we made mistakes in school. I remember one night my chum and I were racing upstairs to see who would be the first to put the lights on. He won *that* race—jumped for the cord and pulled the whole light out, wires and all! He was sent to see the minister, but I don't know what happened to him, because I wasn't there and he never told me.

In the morning, right after breakfast, we'd have lessons in reading, writing, arithmetic, singing, and Bible study. The settlers' children, from the families of white trappers and hunters, were in separate classes from us. They were taught in English, and we spoke Inuktitut. The teacher who taught us Inuktitut was of German descent, and her parents were missionaries in Nain, along with some missionaries from England who ministered to us for a long time. It was our teacher's idea to have the separate classes; we were expected to live as our ancestors did, and learn our own language. But some of us,

We slid down the hills on sealskins or used skis we made oursleves.

myself included, picked up some English when we were older, just by being in contact with white people.

I don't remember our teacher's name, but I do recall her assistant's name—Katie Hedas. She was an English missionary who also spoke Inuktitut. All four of the teachers were missionaries, and we kids would go to church every Sunday, dressed as our ancestors did, in sealskin pants and the white coats we call *silapaak*. These white shells were special Sunday wear, but we wore the sealskin pants every day.

Sealskin was very useful material for Inuit children in the school. We had sleeping bags made from the skins of bedlamer and harp seals, and skins were also great for when we played outside in the winter, after our classes were over for the day. We'd use the skins for sliding—they were made by our mothers and the other Inuit women, and they were so smooth and strong that we could slide really fast and far on them. But sometimes we wouldn't even bother with the skins, just slide down hills on our bottoms. That's why we wore our sealskin pants every day. After a while, there'd be no fur left on the bottoms of our pants from sliding on them too much.

Our boots, too, were made of sealskin. Even on a cold, brisk, wintry day, when we were almost blinded by the sun against the snow, and our boots were frozen stiff, we'd never get cold feet. Our socks always stayed dry under the skin boots, frozen as they were.

Our play was governed by our mood. Soccer is a favourite game among Inuit; often we play it on the sea ice in the winter, even at night—when the moon and stars are out. But some of the boys preferred sliding. So those who wanted to play soccer would play soccer, while others would slide on skins. There weren't any skis available in Nain when I was a child, but we would make them ourselves from barrel staves.

So even though we had no store-bought luxury items, we were
happy, especially sliding down hills.

Sometimes we got into fights, but they were quickly for-
gotten. A child sees and acts quite differently from an adult.
He takes something without thinking, and he is also quick to
forget his anger.

In the winter, we kids were also outside to do the chores
we had every day. The school didn't have a furnace, so after
dinner we would go out to chop wood. Some of us weren't
very experienced, so we weren't able to chop up very much
wood. But we had a good time, and there was never a quiet
moment, especially when we got to the point where we could
chop a lot of wood and make shavings from dry wood to use as
kindling in the morning. Somehow, the shavings always started
flying around when it was just about time to go back inside!

On very cold days, or during a fierce blizzard, we almost
ran out of wood sometimes, and we children would have to
bring in tree branches to burn. Then there was water to fetch.
It took seven of us kids to haul the school's huge water tank
on a sled, back and forth to the well, again and again, the runners of the sled always icing up and slowing us down. What a
lot of work we did!

Christmas Time

Inuit in Labrador really believe in Christmas, and we always travel a long way to get the perfect Christmas tree. When I was growing up, we went by dogsled. There are many trees around Nain, but we would go deep into the woods to find the best one. My family and I decorated our tree with anything we could get, just as most of the families in Nain did. We used coloured paper, shells from the beach, even the molasses candies my mother always made at Christmas time. (There wasn't any candy for sale at the store.)

We attended every church service during the season, from Advent to Christmas Day. The candlelight service on Christmas Eve was the most fun. It was held at four in the afternoon, but in winter the sky was always dark by then, so it was a perfect setting for a candlelight service. Each child received a candle stuck into an apple. The apple represented the world, and the candle was the light of the world. What a beautiful sight it must have been to anyone sitting inside: the children carrying all those lighted candles into the church, so festive with its two big trees and the enormous star hanging from the ceiling. All the while the choir sang, and Inuit accompanied them, reading from their hymnals.

The organist was in charge of the choir. He had to know all the songs, because he led the violinists and the singers. We would have known the difference right away if the choir was not singing in harmony, so they practised many hours before singing in the church. They had a very exacting education. Remember how I told you about the men coming and carrying my father to church so he could play the organ? That was because he was really needed to keep the choir going, so they would sing well. And they did. Our choir was exceptional.

Sometimes people who were dozing in the pews got quite a start when the singers suddenly struck a loud note!

Being a member of the choir or a chapel servant in our church was very important when I was growing up. Those were the people who controlled all church business and all our celebrations, and helped to run the community, along with the elders. Sometimes they raised money for projects like repairing the church organ; they would hold a bingo or something like that. They also helped people who were having personal problems or needed advice about making a difficult decision for their families, like finding someone to foster a child when one of the parents had died. So not just anybody could sing in the choir or be a chapel servant. It was up to the elders, the chapel servants, and the members of the choir to look for new people. They would hold meetings to decide who to recruit, and if the chosen ones agreed, their names were formally noted and they became part of the church elite. Only men could play in the church's brass band, but both men and women were choir members and chapel servants.

One duty the chapel servants had that meant a lot to us kids was collecting Christmas presents for all the children in the community, which sometimes took all year to do. We would get our presents from the minister and the chapel servants at eight o'clock on Christmas Eve, a few hours after the candlelight service. We were always excited walking back to the church in the cold, crisp, winter night, wondering what we were going to get.

The gifts were simple—one year I got a house that I could put together like a puzzle—but we always loved them. Not one child was left out, and that tradition is one we will always hold on to, even though the church is almost too small for all the people who live in Nain now. When I was growing up, there were about three hundred people living here; now there are more than one thousand.

The original church was built in 1771, but it burned down and was rebuilt in 1921. The new church is still standing, and has also been used for a long time by many people. A lot of people have been baptized there, attended Christmas services, gone for their confirmation, gotten married—all of it. Yet there it is. And I think it will stand for a long time yet.

On Christmas Day, the brass band would start playing outside the church at seven in the morning. Even when the weather was extra cold, they had to perform. That was the rule. The band always practised very hard for Christmas morning, because it was so important to all the people. The musicians knew that when they learned a piece thoroughly, they could play it without looking at a score sheet. You can memorize a lot of different hymns in your head. I know this is true from experience. When I got older, I played the violin in the choir and I was also in the brass band, not just at Christ-

It was a great honour for any Inuk to play in the brass band.

mas but for all the festive occasions. Sometimes we played in the church, and sometimes outside, even in storms. But I never minded the weather, because it was an honour to be part of the choir or the band.

There was a very special service on Christmas Day, and I remember it well. The minister always told the story about Jesus being born in Bethlehem of Judea—that he was poor, homeless, and born amongst farm animals in a manger. Those words were both amazing and comforting. The minister talked about things that we could understand personally, and I will never forget them.

After the church service, people would visit each others' homes, bringing gifts of food to those who were unable to hunt for themselves. Always we remember those less fortunate than ourselves.

The choir sang not only at church but for special celebrations throughout the year. Even on the coldest day, they'd gather outside to sing.

A Lot to Learn

When I stopped going to school, I went to live with my mother again. Inuit families lived together in one house—aunts, uncles, cousins, and grandparents. The house was divided into sections for each part of the family.

My mother had remarried, and I lived with her, my stepfather, and his family in one of these households. My uncle and his family were in another section, and my grandparents lived in the third one. Each household had a head person who was in charge of gathering and storing food and managing the money. It was his job to make sure we had enough to eat. In my household, the head person was my stepfather.

My stepfather taught me a lot about how to provide for a family, and there was a lot to learn. He showed me how to jig

We used to go wooding as soon as the first snow fell. We always needed a lot of wood to keep warm all winter.

for cod: some of the fish we would eat fresh, some we would sell, and some would be dried outdoors so that we could store it in barrels for winter eating. He also taught me to hunt for game and seals using a .22-calibre rifle, and to handle a dog

team, which was our only means of winter transportation.

With the help of our dogs, we were able to go hunting, deliver mail, and visit people in other communities. We also went wooding by dogsled to collect the fuel we would need to heat our houses all year, and the firewood we could sell for a dollar a cord. We chopped the wood next to the minister's house; some of the money we earned from it went to buy groceries, but something was always kept for the collection plate.

After a wooding trip, we saved up some of the logs to sell as firewood—but some we kept for ourselves.

The dogs knew their owner; they knew their own names, and they knew how to follow the commands given by the driver. If you wanted them to go ahead, you would shout *"Harra! Harra!"* Dogs have an intelligence, and you can communicate with them through language.

As soon as the snow started falling, we would go wooding on land by dog team while the harbour was still risky. There would be a lot of teams out by then. Some of the dogs were really strong, and you could travel a long distance with them, even on a wooding trail like ours, which was difficult to follow before the snow got packed down. Those dogs went really fast down the slopes in the early days of winter; *they*, at least, enjoyed running in the soft snow! Even in bad weather, the driver and his team could keep moving, as long as the driver knew the land. Even if he didn't, his dogs could always get him home if he was lost in bad weather. I myself have experienced this while I was out wooding.

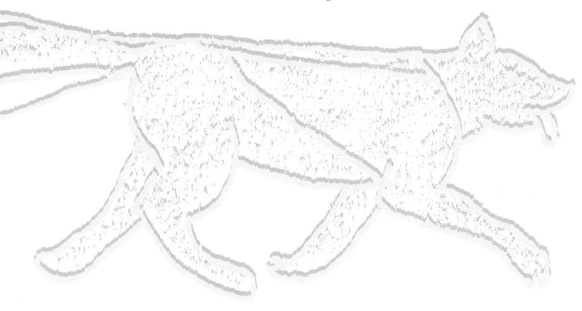

Unlike humans, sled dogs enjoyed running in the soft snow down the slopes in early winter.

You had to be careful on the trail. One time my stepfather and I were returning from wooding, and while we were sliding down a hill, I accidentally dragged my foot. I got thrown way off the sled, which headed straight for me. If my stepfather hadn't acted quickly to jerk the sled away from me, I surely would have died.

My stepfather didn't go to church very much—only when he felt the need. He was always reading the Bible, though, every chance he got. He used to tell me not to be lazy about doing work, because that way I would never own anything, just by being too lazy to work for it. I believed him when he said that, so I'd get up really early to go wooding on my own.

I always returned early, too, when the other dog teams were just getting ready to head out on the trail—but that was for another reason. In those days, the village elders were always telling the children stories about the shamans, or about all the ghosts that were around when they were young. Many of the ghost stories were about bats, and I was very scared of them because I was sure they would swoop down on me and try to gouge out my eyes with their claws. All the other kids were scared of them, too, and we would fall down flat on the ground every time a bat came anywhere near us.

When I first started going off by myself, wooding or hunting, I used to be really nervous and jumpy, thinking that I was being stalked by imaginary bat-demons from the stories I had heard. Once, while I was out wooding, a partridge unexpectedly flew up from the brush. I was so frightened, I think all my hair stood on end!

So that's why I would always hurry when I was first going out wooding or hunting alone, and that's why I would always be back home before the other teams even got started. When I returned, I never told anybody about how scared I'd been. They would have just laughed at me!

Eventually I got over the bat-demons, probably because I liked going out by myself so much. I used to walk all over the hills, looking for partridges or small game. One day when I was out walking, a nice, gentle, westerly breeze was blowing. I was walking along the edge of a lake when I saw something black moving along in the distance. I headed away from the wind and soon saw that it was a porcupine, so I shot it with my .22. But when I went to skin the porcupine, I discovered that I didn't have my knife. I was really afraid of the quills, but I had to lug the whole thing home on my back anyway. Whenever it felt like one of those needles was going into my back, I quickly examined myself in panic—but I managed to get home without being stabbed. I skinned it after lunch.

When my stepfather saw what I was doing, he asked me if I had been carrying a knife while I was out hunting. I had to confess that I had not brought one. He didn't get angry, but simply explained to me that whenever I went hunting, I should always make sure that I carried everything I would need—an axe, a .22 with ammunition, and a knife.

Inuit Games

Another way we learned to become good hunters was by playing games. They were like exercises or stunts that were for building muscles; all the muscles in our bodies had to be in shape in order for us to do the work we had to do. When we were children, some of us were so flexible that we seemed double-jointed, while others seemed too shy even to try to do anything. We were always told not to hold back from trying the exercises, because they would make us successful hunters in later years.

Our teacher was John Bennett, who ran the gym classes at the mission school I attended when I was a boy. He knew all kinds of games, and he did a good job of instructing us. Often we would gather at his house, sometimes staying for hours on end when there were a lot of us trying to beat each other. Even when we didn't know how to do a certain exercise, we'd keep on trying and catch on eventually. One exercise that was very hard involved stretching your legs out stiffly in front of you while holding yourself up by

The Inuk in this picture (below) will have very strong teeth, jaws, and neck from doing this exercise.

one arm from a rope tied to one of the ceiling rafters. The rope was made from square flipper skin or harp-seal skin with a wooden handle on the end. In another one, a young man would hang by his teeth from a rope hooked onto a piece of wood. He would do this to strengthen his teeth, jaws, and neck, because there would come a time when he had to be able to throw a seal aboard a boat with just his teeth.

The Inuk who tried this next exercise had to be very careful. What he tried to do was hang by his feet with his hands crossed behind his head. He got into this position by hanging onto a rope with his hands, bringing his feet up to a stick above his head, then letting his body hang upside down with his hands held behind his head. After that, he had to return to the original position by lifting his body up without letting go with his feet. Sometimes we kids would fall to the floor trying to do this trick. Your feet had to have a really good grip.

We also played many games on the floor—like the monkey-dance, which we called "Learning how to Run" because people said that those who could monkey-dance the longest could run the fastest. There were two ways of doing the monkey-dance, one with only your heels hitting the floor, the other with only your toes touching down. Either way, your legs had to be bent very deeply. The one who got tired first always lost the game: either he would just have to stop, or he would fall over when he tried to dance. This game really helped us strengthen our leg muscles, and some guys who had been doing it for a while could monkey-dance for a very long time. Some could go more than two hundred times without stopping, and some could even put on and take off their dickies—those are like duffel coats without zippers—while they were doing the dance.

Some guys could monkey-dance more than two hundred times without stopping.

Then there were competitions. We would put a belt around the necks of two guys who were facing each other, and then they'd try to pull each other over. Your neck and arms had to be very strong in order for you to compete in this game; otherwise you would be pulled over right away. Some people were so strong that they could haul another person around like a rag doll. They would make very good seal hunters.

Another game I thought was a lot of fun was a contest between two guys who had to hold their left leg with their left hand while using the right hand to balance the full weight of the body. Then they bumped each other's shoulder, trying to knock their opponent down or make them release his foot. The first one down lost, and you didn't always lose just because the other guy bumped your shoulder; it was easy to lose your balance and drop your foot down when you aimed for his shoulder but missed.

Some people were so strong that they could drag an opponent around like a rag doll. These Inuit are more evenly matched.

There were a lot of other Inuit floor games, like the one where two people held a stick between them while they were sitting across from each other, then tried to pull each other over. You had to keep your legs straight, too. This exercise was very good for the arms, the neck, and the legs. Your hands also had to be strong, so that you could keep your grip on the stick. If you let go, you lost the game. We were always taught to use all our strength when we were playing this game, because that way we would know exactly how powerful we were.

Sometimes the young men and women would play games together. It was fun and embarrassing at the same time. When I was a young man, accordions were becoming popular, and we would play a game similar to musical chairs, which we called "Competing for a Seat." We would start out with the girls seated on the chairs. When the music stopped, the boys would have to hurry and find a lap to sit on. Whoever was left standing had to kiss a girl he liked, and then the game would start all over again, with the boys on the chairs this time.

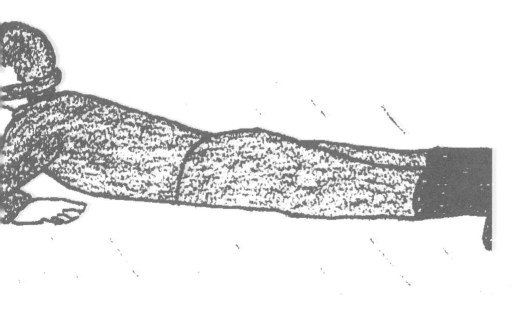

There was another game called "Rabbit," in which the boys and girls teamed up. If the boy was the rabbit, his partner would run after him between two lines of players, females on one side and males facing their partners. When she caught him, she became the rabbit, and he chased her. The game would continue until everyone had a turn.

We all enjoyed playing these games—even the ones where one person was blindfolded and had to chase the others. The one who was caught would then have a turn playing the "blind man." This game kind of gave me the creeps, whether I was playing or just watching from the sidelines. It always felt like I was the only one being chased. But after a while, it got to be fun, in a scary sort of way.

I could go on and on about all the games we played at John Bennett's house. He and his wife, Sybella, gave us a lot of joy. They had just been married when we first started going over there, but later on they had many children. After John died, his son Gustave followed in his father's steps, organizing and participating in many sports, like baseball in the spring and hockey in the winter.

Gustave died on a caribou-hunting trip in 1978, which was a very cold winter. I was in the search party that was sent from Nain to look for him. My wife's son from a previous marriage came along with us, but he got lost while we were out there, and we never found the body. Those two tragic deaths were a terrible lesson in how unforgiving this land can be.

Labrador is
beautiful, but
the land can be
harsh and
unforgiving—
and it can claim
life as easily as it
sustains life.

The First Time I Shot a Caribou

My stepfather and I hunted rabbits, foxes, and caribou in the woods and on the barren-lands of northern Labrador. Caribou were only in the barrens, and for seals, of course, you had to be on the coast. Going hunting inland wasn't just an easy game or sport. Sometimes it was stormy for a long time, and

the middle of the winter, in January, it isn't wise to go out hunting if the weather looks as if it might act up. The weather has a destructive force all its own, and you can get really high winds in the winter.

Some Inuit know the barren-lands like the palm of their hand. They know where the foxes' dens are, and where the best hunting places are. They know how to look after themselves up there. Some Labrador men who are old men now still know how to survive in this very different kind of environment. I remember some of the stories these old men told me, the real fox-trappers who used to go far inland and stay in the country for long periods of time. They would get many fox skins, which they would sell for very high prices in those days. The older men would even go wooding when they were heading into the country. That was the only way to get a hot meal, because there are no trees in the high barren-lands. When they ran out of wood, they used candles to boil water.

These were lessons that were passed from generation to generation. Our trips were much shorter—about two weeks—but when I first began caribou hunting, we always chopped wood to bring along for the part of the trip that would take us past the edge of the tree line. We also learned very quickly that anyone who is travelling long distances by dogsled must carry snowshoes; they are a very important part of a hunter's gear. When you're using a dog team, the drifts can be piled very high on the trail by the rivers after it has been snowing for some time. The deep snow can stop you completely, so you have to keep clearing your trail with the snowshoes.

Anyone who is going on a hunting trip by dogsled always carries snowshoes.

It's very frustrating when you have to keep stopping on the trail to free the runners of the sled fron wet, sticky snow.

There are many hardships during winter hunting, even when the weather is fine. You can go snow-blind, especially in the barrens, where there is nothing to break the glare of sun on snow. The wind cam be damaging to the eyes, too. The snow gets covered with a thin layer of frost, and the wind blows this hoar-frost around.

A wet snowfall can also make it really hard going for you. The wet snow sticks to the runners of the sled and can cause you a lot of grief. Then your clothes get wet from having to bend down and free the runners from the sticky snow all the time. Sometimes you can get very wet and hungry, and when your stomach is empty as well as your clothes being soaked, your body quickly loses its heat, because it has nothing to regenerate itself with. That's how a person can die.

Some Inuit find it too time-consuming to stop and eat while they are travelling, even when they are feeling hunger pangs. But our attitude was that while an Inuk has breath in him, he must try to stay alive in any way that he can. Let him stop and eat, we would say; the meat will not taste old as long as there is flour to make gravy. And even those who have not hunted will receive their share of the kill.

When Inuit are hunting, they believe in working together. Some build snow houses and some hunt. A snow house, or igloo, is built from the inside out. First, blocks of snow are cut and a place to build the snow house is marked on the ground. Then, one person stands in the middle of where the house is to be built and places the blocks on top of each other; the last block is the roof. The people outside the snow house fill the cracks with packed snow and smooth the surface of the walls. When all the cracks are covered and it is totally dark inside, the person in the house cuts open a doorway. When the house is built, we share our food.

An igloo, or snow house, is built from the inside out, block by block.

The first time I went caribou hunting by dogsled, there were three teams of us heading inland. Every day this young guy and I were ahead of the other teams, breaking the trail and scouting. We had no idea which way we were supposed to go; our head man would just tell us to travel towards the lowest hills, and we'd take off each morning while the others were finishing the packing.

One day, when we had been travelling for six days, we spied fresh caribou tracks. So I began to follow them, while my companion continued to lead the teams. Suddenly, I noticed that the dogs were headed in another direction, far inland away from where I was following the tracks. I didn't want to be stranded, so I began chasing the other hunters, running all the way because they were already quite a distance from me. I was sweating all over when I finally caught up with them. We walked all day without stopping, the young guy and I continuing to break the trail. The dogs got so far behind us that sometimes we couldn't even see them, so we'd have to wait for the others in order to find out which way to go. But we weren't suffering. We were enjoying ourselves, because we were young and didn't let a few annoyances get to us.

We were already high in the barren-lands, a long way from Nain, when we saw a man from another hunting party that had been inland for a long time without catching a single caribou. The guy talked with our boss, who said we would be returning to Nain the next day, so it was decided that his group would join ours. Some of the other hunters were still far behind; we were having breakfast early the next morning when they arrived. When we had finished packing, we all headed out together, as a party of seven teams.

You have to be careful staring at the sun on the snow in the barren-lands, because it can badly damage your eyes.

It was blowing a little and snowing lightly when we started out, but then gale-force winds came in from the north, blowing so fiercely that the sky became dark. Just then our dogs began catching a scent on the wind: they started galloping, then slowed almost to a standstill, sniffed the wind, and started running again, getting more and more excited. The older hunters decided we should stop.

We sighted caribou! Everyone started shooting, and it sounded like the bullets were hitting their targets. You can hear the thud when a bullet hits its mark; you don't hear the report when it goes astray. And these shots could be heard.

There were twenty caribou, and we shot sixteen.

We were happy then, and I was especially happy, because I had shot my first caribou.

We sighted the caribou the day before we were supposed to start home from our hunting trip.

The next morning we were homeward bound, but it took a bit longer than usual to come down from Tasitsuak because of the deep, soft snow. I was getting really exhausted from walking through soft snow, but we had to make up time, so we ended up travelling nights.

We reached Nain about two in the morning, so I had to knock on the window to wake the household. I was so sleepy that I kept saying *"Huit!"* while I was unharnessing the dogs, even though we weren't going anywhere. Even inside, talking to my parents, I kept saying *"Huit!"* When my stepfather asked if I was tired, I had to say yes. No wonder; it was my first caribou-hunting trip.

I was so tired after my first caribou-hunting trip that I kept on giving commands to the dogs even after I unharnessed them.

Along with the caribou, I also shot five foxes. When day dawned, my stepfather cleaned my foxes for me; later, they would be sold to the manager at the Hudson's Bay Company store. Then we all sat down to a feast of caribou meat, cooked by my mother. I was home! It was time to relax and enjoy the meat.

Special Days

The Labrador Inuit have many other wintertime celebrations besides Christmas. From the time our ancestors began to attend schools and churches, festive days have been a tradition that, in my day, we regarded as a major cultural event. Just about everyone had their own special day to celebrate, and they would always go to church to mark the occasion. The brass band and choir performed for them. They wore special boots with fancy fur leggings, which the women made just for the holidays. They stopped whatever they were working at, took a rest, and shared a feast.

Other times of the year, the people lived as they could, through very difficult times, and through times of great joy. But once a year, people celebrated their special day.

The first festivity of the year was held during the coldest month—January. This was Young Man's Day, which was for boys over the age of twelve and young single men. All the young men held a meeting first, as everything had to be planned carefully so that there was no doubt in anyone's mind what he was expected to do to help organize the festivities. During the meeting we would decide exactly when the special day would be held and in whose house we would meet early on the chosen Young Men's Day.

The morning before our celebration, we would go hunting for game to enjoy the next day. We were more likely to find the rabbits, partridges, and porcupines we wanted by going a good distance from the community, so we always travelled by dogsled. Then, at six the next morning, we'd go to the house where we had agreed to meet and have breakfast together. Some years, there'd be a lot of bachelors, and we would have to arrange for two guest houses!

Young men head over to the church after sharing breakfast at their guest house.

After breakfast, at nine o'clock, the young men went to church, where the flags had been raised on the official flagstaff. The brass band and the choir would perform for the young men who had just turned thirteen and were being initiated into adulthood. At the end of the day, these young men were congratulated by the whole choir and band.

The celebration is both solemn and beautiful, and although it is not as common a tradition now as it was when I was a young man, it is one that Inuit will never give up entirely.

Widows had their special day on February 2. When I was growing up, life was full of physical hardships for Inuit, and the men often died of illness or were lost in the woods. Their widows were very lonely after having been through such hardships by their husbands' side, and they experienced new worries, too, with children to care for on their own. Life was no longer the same for them, and although there was nothing anyone could do to bring their husbands back, the people were able to help these widows with all the things they could not do themselves, like hunting and wooding.

This happened throughout the year, but on Widows' Day it was something extra: everyone ran errands for them and acted like their servants all day long. The young men brought them special gifts of game, chopped wood, and fetched water. The highlight of the day came when the widows met in their guest house, where they had a feast of seal meat, presented to them by the men.

On Widows' Day, the young men chopped extra wood and did many other chores for the women celebraing their special day.

February 19 was a very special church day, celebrated by the whole congregation. It marked the beginning of the church in Labrador, many years ago. On that day, the first convert to the church, an *angakkuk* named Qimminguuse, was baptized. *Angakkuk* is the Inuit word for shaman, and this particular shaman was apparently so powerful that he could kill his enemy without even touching him. He had no use for a knife, or any other weapon; he just used his special powers. So when Inuit heard that someone as powerful as Qimminguuse was becoming a Christian, they too began to convert to the church.

Married couples had their day on February 28. First they went to church, where the minister talked to them about how they should live their lives. He would say that married people should help each other to make things easier. Life can be a heavy burden when you are bothered by the temptations the world holds in front of you. Ugliness can begin to rule your life. It is best to try to stay happy with the people in your life, he would say, and I have to agree.

There were also special days for children and older people. Little girls and boys spent their day at a guest house, where they had a big dinner and supper, then went to church for what was called a love feast—a cup of tea and a bun. At church, the girls and women wore a *nasatsuk*, a white knitted cap with red ribbons for the women and pink for the girls. They also wore these caps to the candlelight service on Christmas Eve.

We also celebrated each Inuk's fiftieth birthday, as a way of honouring the wisdom of older people. When someone turned fifty, the brass band and choir would assemble outside their house and perform for them.

March 6 was Young Women's Day. It was always cold—as anyone knows who ever played in the brass band or sang in the choir and had to be outside their guest house at seven in the morning! Like the young men, girls over thirteen and unmarried women spent their day at someone's house and had a feast. They attended two special services, and there was always a long line of girls and women marching in single file to the church and back.

En route to church on Young Women's Day, March 6.

Cod Fishing

The government-run freight boat came to Labrador every
year, delivering foodstuffs to all the communities: Hebron,
Nutak, Nain, Davis Inlet, Hopedale, Makkovik, and Postville.
This schooner and its captain were well known to the people.
The older Inuit knew its history and its ventures, that it travelled
through storms, through fog, through high seas at the capes and
at barren points of land that are cliff and mountain.

For the people of Nain, the first sight of the schooner
meant spring break-up had come, and we could soon move
out to our cod-fishing places outside Nain—Killisuak,
Aupalattuk, and Kikittaujak. My stepfather, his son, Samuel,
and I fished from a punt, which is a fair-sized rowboat. In
those days, many people who only had rowboats were taken
out to their fishing places by those who owned motorboats.
This was another way Inuit helped each other. But my family
usually rowed from Nain, setting out at four in the morning.
Our old man liked to get up early.

When the
government
freight boat
made its way
into Nain, we
knew that
spring break-
up had finally
come.

Sometimes, if a breeze was blowing in the right direction, we would set up our sails. What relaxation! No more rowing; the wind would send us speeding along. But the wind can change without warning, and if it dropped, we would have to use all our strength to manage the sails, or switch back to the oars. It was hard work, but we never got disheartened because we knew that once we got there, we'd soon be enjoying a feast of fresh cod.

My stepfather never let us go hungry. We'd be filling up the old punt three times a day with codfish—and we wouldn't have to wait long to have a taste. As soon as we had our first load, we would split the fish, salt it down in barrels, then cook up fresh cod we had set aside for ourselves. What a treat!

My stepfather used to like to get up very early to go cod-jigging. Usually we had to row to our fishing grounds.

After we had eaten, we would take off jigging again. When you jig for fish, you lower a line with shiny hooks on it to the depth where the cod like to swim. Then you tease the fish by jerking the hooks around to make them think there's food in front of them. I guess it's called jigging because of the motion those hooks make, kind of like dancing a jig. As soon as you feel a bite, you haul up the cod. Some of those fish were really big, and they would put up quite a fight. By the end of the day, our hands would be all blistered, sometimes even bleeding.

My stepfather taught Samuel and me how to use a line with shiny hooks on it to jig for cod in the spring and summer.

Fishermen with
bigger boats
could get a lot of
cod by using
traps.
Sometimes we
accompanied the
Newfoundland
fishermen out to
where their
traps were cast.

Some Inuit who had big motorboats used cod traps, large
square pieces of fishnet that were held by buoys at the corners,
creating a bowl shape below the water. They could fill four
motorboats with cod, using just one trap. There were cod
traps everywhere, not just used by Inuit, but by Newfoundland fishermen who came to the area in their schooners every
year, sometimes twice a year if they were in smaller schooners.
They even tried to arrive early enough in the season to get the
best fishing berths. What a lot of fish was picked up in Labrador by the Newfoundlanders! And the Labrador people never
once tried to stand in their way.

But they were okay, those *kallonat* from the Newfoundland fishing boats. (*Kallonat* means "white people" in
Inuktitut.) They treated us well, so even though there was a
language barrier, we spent quite a bit of time together. We

would visit their schooners and sometimes go to their traps with them, sharing a meal afterwards.

There would be a lot of merrymaking in the evening when they came ashore. They didn't have accordions, but they used makeshift music-makers for their dances. These were like mouth organs, made by putting a piece of paper over a comb. I'll never forget one man, Philip, who could play an amazing jig on one of these crude instruments just by imitating the sounds of the notes. Now *there* was a man whose mouth didn't have stiff muscles!

Another good thing about going cod fishing in those days was that there was always enough fish for everyone. Many people would stay out at their fishing places all spring and summer, setting up camps and even building little houses. The freight boat delivered store-bought orders to our fishing camps when it came in to pick up our catch during the season, but once in a while the manager refused to send goods to the fishermen, so they'd have to go to Nain to pick up their orders. That was a real difficulty for anyone who had to row there and back; it was a four-hour trip each way.

Many Inuit families built little cabins at their cod-fishing places, and stayed all summer.

For other Inuit fishermen, even the end of the season—the early fall, when we got paid for our catch—was a disappointment. They would be expecting at least *some* cash to show for all their hard work, but often they would show up at the store in Nain only to find out that the value of their season's catch had only gone towards paying off part of what they owed on their account. Some of these men had large families, and the situation at the store was hard for them to accept. And it didn't make things any easier when some of the managers were rude to them for no other reason, it seemed, than that they spoke no English.

Tallying up a season's catch at the store in the early fall.

Still, with the cod so plentiful, there was always enough to eat; no one was starving. In my day, there was quite a bit of rock cod in the waters around Nain as early in the season as late winter or the beginning of spring. We used to dry or freeze these tasty fish, or, better still, have a feast of fish and brewis, which is a stew made of the cod, salt pork, onions, and hard bread that has been soaked in water. My parents were great cooks, and this was one of our favourite meals.

But there don't seem to be many cod left these days. I tried to go cod fishing one summer just a couple of years ago, but all I got was char and sea trout, even though I went a long distance—from Nain to Rama. The fishermen I spoke to who did get some cod said the fish were very small. I don't know why there are so few cod left, but a lot of us think that over-fishing is the cause.

There has also been a lot of talk about the Japanese and Russian trawlers that were dragging in the waters for cod, and how they might have destroyed the spawning and feeding grounds for the cod. That's what we heard, anyway.

Easter and the Coming of Spring

During Easter week, we weren't allowed to leave the community to go hunting or wooding, so we tried to have all that work done before Easter came around. Even children weren't supposed to be rowdy, or even go sliding. Inuit ways of keeping holy days are practised to this day by many people. The only difference from the time when we were children is that there are fewer restrictions.

The chapel servants were always in charge of Easter celebrations, even those that took place outdoors. We celebrated all week. Easter morning we went to church at four-thirty; then the brass band would lead the congregation to the graveyard. We always tried to be there when the sun rose. It was a time to remember the meaning of Easter—that Christ had sacrificed himself for us—and it was a time to think about people who had died.

When Easter was over, spring began. In the early spring, Inuit would saw up lumber for making sleds, sled bars, and flats, and we would repair the wharves that had been damaged by the fierce winter storms. Inuit always helped each other when they were sawing wood to make these necessary articles of our trade. We worked together happily without ever thinking of asking for money from our fellow Inuit.

The more experienced men only taught the younger Inuit how things were to be done, how things are made. An Inuk also had to learn for himself, through first-hand experience. Work like that wasn't so difficult—sawing your own lumber with a handsaw. The worst thing that happened was that your arm got tired and you sweated a lot. The real lesson we learned from the older people was how to work co-operatively and in an organized fashion.

The older people taught younger Inuit how things were done, but you had to learn through experience, too.

We were always happy to finally shed our winter clothing—even though spring also meant lots of hard work—like raking grass.

As soon as the snow melted in the early spring, all the Inuit would join together to clean up the community grounds. Called to our work by the church bell, we would rake the grass and pick up the garbage. When the land began to turn green, it was truly beautiful to see. I even loved the smell, unpolluted by garbage—the true smell of the land, the earth, the fresh air, the growing things.

We would spend all Sunday outdoors, walking around relaxed, looking at the mountains and the land. The long days and the warm sun always made me feel glad just to know I had survived another winter of cutting down trees just to stay alive in the bad storms and the sub-zero weather we endured in the inland caribou-hunting ground.

Everywhere I looked, all kinds of living things were beginning to thrive again. Robins, sparrows, and many other small birds sang in the early morning, their harmonies as beautiful as music. The bigger game birds began to appear, too—eider ducks, geese, black ducks—and, of course, those scavengers, the seagulls! At least their eggs were worth keeping. Along with pigeons' eggs, they were the tastiest of the ones we collected in the early spring. We got ducks' eggs, too, but they had a slightly stronger taste.

Not that finding any of those eggs was easy. Wild birds' eggs can't just be picked up like stones; they're tucked away in some pretty inaccessible spots. Sometimes you have to do some cliff-climbing with a strong rope, then use a long piece of wire to pull them out from under the big overhanging rocks where birds hide them. But we didn't mind making the effort, because we knew this was the only time we would be eating eggs. Eggs were yet another item on the long list of things you couldn't buy at the store.

Another way we celebrated the coming of spring was by having a picnic out at Nain Point. After lunch, the children, young men, and married couples began setting up the bases for a game of baseball. A lot of people would gather together, showing their kids how to play ball and have fun. It was a great holiday after a long, cold winter.

Getting gulls' eggs was no easy task, but the hunt was worthwhile because spring was the only time we ever got to eat eggs.

Seal Hunting

At the very first sign of spring break-up, our thoughts turned to the seal hunt at the edge of the ice floe. It would be some time before the water was sufficiently free of ice to start moving out to the cod-fishing places, but we could get to our seal-hunting grounds by land in the very early spring.

It's always best to go and see for yourself what the hunting grounds look like. Sometimes there isn't any open water beyond the floe edge, for ice forms quickly if there is no wind, and frosty weather slows down the break-up. You also have to watch out for fierce spring storms in the countryside around Nain. Mighty gales can create a mass of waves out of the great expanse of water.

The weather destroys when it wants to. No one can stop it. A person can become angry and frustrated at the weather, but he cannot placate it. But the weather is sometimes kind in the early spring, and then Inuit hunters set up camps at their hunting places.

All around Nain there were small houses at these hunting places, and my family had a cabin at Evilik. We felt refreshed just to be there, and wild game wasn't hard to find. It's best to live on the land if you can, because you never go hungry if you are close to your food supply.

My family's cabin at Evilik, our seal-hunting place near Nain.

We always travelled by dog team; that was the only form of transportation we had. Because we used dogs, we were able to get more seals than people do now. The seals weren't disturbed by the dogs and sleds the way they are by the noisy snowmobiles that are used today. There were also more seals then because people didn't over-hunt. Inuit knew the habits of the seals, and they conducted themselves accordingly. They knew that when there had been a heavy snowfall over the winter, few seals would be seen early in the spring. Only when the snow settled would they start coming around in large numbers.

The dogs would sense when something was about to happen; they would start sniffing around even before the seals appeared. That's when the hunters began taking notice. They knew that for sure there was something around—if not seals, then game. So they would move back from the shore to look out to sea and have something to eat. From a high hill, you could look way out to sea. Even if there wasn't any open water, you could sometimes see the odd seal basking by its breathing hole.

If the weather was fine, we would get up really early in the morning to look for basking seals near the open sea. When the hunt was over, the seals were brought in by dog team. The dogs weren't used while the actual hunting was going on, because the vibrations of the runners through the thin ice at the floe edge would have travelled through the water and scared the seals away.

Sometimes I climbed the hill overlooking the open water to see if there were any seals around.

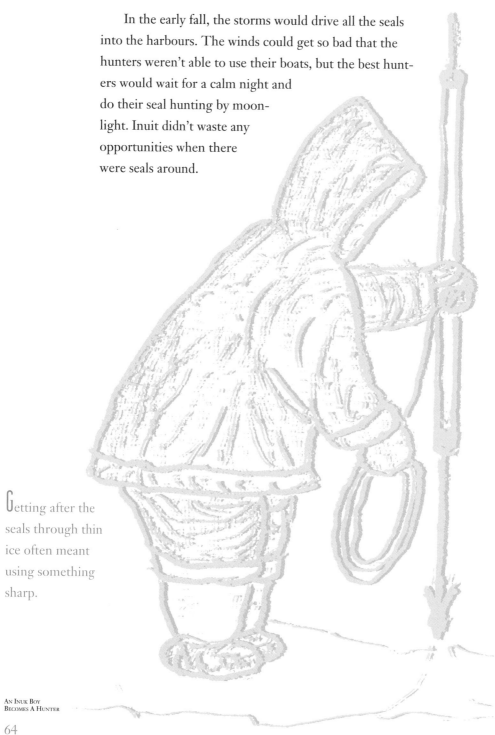

In the early fall, the storms would drive all the seals into the harbours. The winds could get so bad that the hunters weren't able to use their boats, but the best hunters would wait for a calm night and do their seal hunting by moonlight. Inuit didn't waste any opportunities when there were seals around.

Getting after the seals through thin ice often meant using something sharp.

Seals were always plentiful when the thin ice appeared in early winter, and Inuit hunters would be out all over the place. The seals were everywhere, looking for breathing holes at open spots in the thin ice, and the hunters would get up while it was still dark to go and wait for them at the breathing holes. When a group of seals came up at the same time, it was hard to figure out which one to shoot at, there were so many of them. I'd be running around after them with my .22 all day, but I never got tired, maybe because I knew that if we got enough seals, there would be meat to eat all winter.

Sometimes the hunting continued right into the winter. The ice would be seven feet thick, but you could easily make a fishing hole with a sharp auger. In Labrador we have a game regulation that there is to be no hunting on religious holidays, but some years that was a problem for us—the ice was often still thin around Christmas. Inuit did what they had to do to survive, although we always tried to respect the holidays.

After the hunt is over, the dog team will be brought to the floe edge to collect the seals.

Seals were very important to Inuit. Besides for the meat that kept us going through the winter months, we used the blubber for oil and the skins and flippers for clothing, boots, and bedding. We also sold the frozen blubber to the blubber yard in Nain, where it was pounded and then cooked in a big copper pot. The rendered seal oil was stored in drums and shipped out on schooners.

Sealskins had no market value when I was growing up, but they were very useful to us. All winter the women worked at the skins, cleaning them and taking the fur off. For this task they used a narrow wooden cleaning board, a tub to soak the skins, and an *ulu*, which is a woman's knife. They hung the skins outdoors for a while, so that the sun and wind would cure them: only then could they be dried thoroughly and used to make sleeping bags, clothing, boots, and other necessities.

Sealskins were pounded and dried to be made into clothing and boots, while the blubber was stored in barrels and sold.

Square flipper skins were made into lines and ropes or used as dog harnesses after being cut into long, narrow strips. The women also used the flipper skins for the bottoms of boots. All the types of seals were used to make boots. Harp-seal skins were used primarily for the boots we wore every day, while the skins of jar and ranger seals, with the fur left on, were made into the leggings for boots we wore on special occasions. The top part of the boot had elaborate designs in fur, while the bottom, made either of harp or bedlamer skins, was left bare. It was amazing that the women could create such intricate designs just by using different kinds of skins.

Old Ways, Good and Bad

Inuit had to be very resourceful back when I was a child and a young man. They made full use of their skills and knowledge, and helped each other with whatever came up, knowing that they would receive the same helping hand themselves if the need arose. The spirit of co-operation touched every aspect of our lives—raising children, hunting for food, caring for the less fortunate, building houses—and made us a very close-knit people.

We even had to look after many of our medical needs, because no doctors or nurses lived in Nain or any of the nearby communities at that time. There was a travelling doctor who was sent around Labrador by a missionary group, and everybody in Nain looked forward to seeing him, because he would go to people's houses to treat them if they were sick. His name was Dr. Paddon.

The people in Nain also respected him because he would travel by dogsled in the middle of winter to come and help us. Unfortunately, he could only come a couple of times a year, and it wasn't until many years later that a doctor came to live

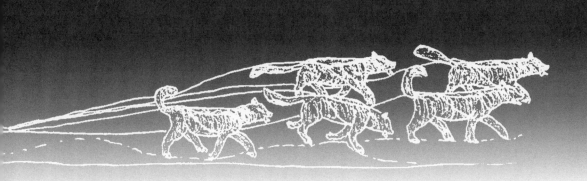

here permanently—Dr. Montgomery. So much of the time, people had to help each other. A lot of people really suffered when the mumps and German measles came around. I remember one year when it seemed like everybody was coming down with the German measles; they had fevers, and red spots all over their bodies. They were really sick. I went to a lot of houses to chop wood that winter, because many people were just too weak to get out of bed for weeks on end.

Inuit women would help each other when they were pregnant, and the older women acted as midwives when the baby was ready to be delivered. Even if a pregnant woman was at the family's campsite during a hunting trip, one of the older women would come to help her if she was about to have the baby.

Sometimes the missionaries would help to look after people who were sick, and if anybody broke a leg or an arm, Johannes Green, one of the white settlers, would set it for them. We thought highly of these people, because they believed in the same spirit of co-operation as we did.

Dr. Paddon was highly thought of by Inuit in Nain—he travelled by dogsled to visit our community.

The young couple watch happily as the minister prepares to baptize their baby. The woman holding the child is a chapel servant.

Inuit also appreciated the significance of the church in the community. The church served a useful function, not just by organizing the festivities, but by encouraging people to live better lives and offer help to one another.

One practice of the church that we value very highly is the baptism of children. When I was younger, babies were always baptized after the ten o'clock Sunday morning service, when the minister was finished delivering the sermon. One of the female chapel servants would hold the newborn baby while the minister blessed the child, speaking the name chosen by the parents. After the baptism, the minister would talk about the way children should be raised. He would say that we should not expose young and impressionable children to bad habits, because they might grow up believing this was an acceptable way to live.

These were beliefs we shared, and it was good for young couples to hear the minister express them. I remember two ministers in particular, Rev. Hettasch and Rev. Peacock, who were very well liked by people in Nain. They moved away some time ago, but the mission houses where they lived are still standing. I don't think the houses are as old as the church, but they're pretty old, anyway.

The elders of the community also did a lot to guide the young people, in some ways maybe even more than the church did. Some of the older men and women taught me a great deal about how to live a happy and fulfilling life. At the time, I only nodded my head, as if it didn't matter, but it did sink in. I was taught how to live my life in harmony; I was taught not to be lazy about doing work and making things with my hands. I was taught not to steal from others, because stealing would only make me poorer. And I was taught that while I hunted, I would be given the animals I needed by God.

I believed all those sayings of the old men and women because they always proved to be right. Although I strayed from them to some extent, later in life, I eventually returned to the truths that had been offered to me by elders like Isaac Rich, who used to talk to me a lot when I was a young man. He spoke from experience, and I will always remember him.

Inuit did live co-operatively with many of the white people in Labrador, like the missionaries, doctors, and settlers. But those of us who grew up in Nain in those days know all too well how the people used to be treated by many of the company store managers. These managers refused to order lumber for us to build our houses, or to order boats that would allow us to pursue cod fishing more effectively—not to mention any little extras, like treats for the children. Sometimes they were not even any clothes or groceries for sale—

Inuit believed
in working
together to
accomplish
their goals—
and they
still do.

and if there were, we couldn't afford them. If a single apple costs fifty cents and you are earning ten cents an hour, you aren't going to be buying apples at the store very often.

So we would work together to saw up boards for a house; we would repair our old punts for the next fishing season. The clothing would be made by the women; the food would be hunted by the men. We would even plant some fruits and vegetables to enjoy in the summer.

We would have appreciated some help from these store managers to at least try to ease the hardships of our way of life, but at least we were able to survive by making use of our own resources and drawing strength from those who believed in the spirit of co-operation, Inuit and white people alike.

However, it was difficult to ignore some of the attitudes the store managers demonstrated in their dealings with Inuit people. I remember things like a manager insisting on only selling us five cartridges at a time, instead of a box of twenty—as if he thought Inuit hunters could only be trusted with a few cartridges for their guns. And one time I saw another manager throw an Inuit man out of the store because he asked why there wasn't any food for sale. Other Inuit related similar incidents to me, even involving negative comments about our language and culture. At the time these things were going on, I didn't know that we were dealing with prejudice, but as I got older, I began to realize that it was.

It is important for young people to know how harmful prejudice is. Prejudice can cause people to become very discouraged about themselves, and it can sow the seeds of hatred between people of different cultures—people who have the potential to live together in harmony. Once inflicted, the damage caused by prejudice is not easily repaired, but it is my belief that it is always possible to try.

The store manager used to live in the house up there on the left; the high building was the old storage shed, and next to it was the store. These buildings have all been torn down since I was young.

A New Life

One evening I was talking to an acquaintance of mine who lived in Nain with his wife. He happened to mention that his wife had a sister in Makkovik. Then, out of nowhere, he said, "You should marry my wife's younger sister."

I was completely taken aback. I didn't know this man very well, and even now that I was a grown man, my childhood shyness persisted around people I wasn't used to. So I told him that I didn't have any idea what to say about his suggestion.

He said that he would help me if I wanted to meet the young lady, and he seemed sincere, so I gave it some thought and then told him, "I have no way of getting over to Makkovik."

His response was that we could all go there in his motor-boat—he, my mother, and I—after stopping to visit people in Hopedale. And that's just what we did. I had an uncle in Hopedale, who we stayed with, and then we continued on to Makkovik.

After I met my new girlfriend, Dina, I stayed with her and her grandparents for a while. Dina, her grandparents, my uncle, my mother, and I then returned to Nain so the two families could spend some time together in our home. This was a tradition in the families of young people who were courting.

When it came time for Dina to return to Makkovik, I followed her back there and stayed at her house all through the fall, until her grandparents told me I had to leave. They didn't explain why, but I know now that it was because we were together without being married. After I was sent away from my girlfriend's house, I went to live next door with a couple who were very good people; they were chapel servants. During this time I was going hunting and also earning money by helping to build houses.

In the evenings, Dina would come to see me, and we would go out together. But I didn't know how long we would be able to keep seeing each other, even though I had come to love her very much, and she felt the same way. I was afraid that I was going to lose her completely after being kicked out of her house. Then, one day during the winter, I was invited over to her grandparents' house.

When I went inside, I saw that the whole family was gathered together. It seemed to take them a long time, but they finally told me that Dina and I could get married. The man I had been staying with had talked to the minister about us, and the minister had convinced her grandparents to allow us to be married by telling them we really loved each other and hadn't understood that we were doing anything wrong. When I heard that, I was so relieved that my whole life seemed lightened.

I wanted to be married in church, but my fiancée's grandmother said we shouldn't, because we had been living together like married people before saying our vows. So we were married at the minister's house, on February 4, 1963. At first we lived with Dina's grandparents, but we had plans for a house of our own.

Dina and I were married at the minister's house in Makkovik on February 4, 1963.

Hunting—And a Home

As soon as open water came in spring, Dina and I took off
with a friend of ours, Joe Millik, to go seal hunting. His wife
came too. It was May, and we had beautiful travelling weather
as we headed to Kogaluk, which is south of Makkovik. We
carried all our supplies in our speedboat, including six drums
of oil for the two-cylinder Acadia engine. The water is very
rough around the cape, and the waves are very high; if you fall
overboard, there isn't much chance of saving you. So we had
to be very careful going around the cape.

We set up camps wherever the seals were plentiful;
following the seals, as always, was the way the Inuit hunted. At
first, although we saw seals every day, we couldn't go after them
because of the high winds. But when the weather finally cleared,
in early June, we had quite a catch.

On that hunting trip, I learned a lot more about the habits
of ranger seals—when the young ones are born, how soon
they learn to stay underwater like their mothers, and where
they congregate and travel. I discovered that the more experienced seals stay submerged when they are being hunted in
shallow water, and wait for the boats to pass. Some of them
swim very fast without coming up for air, and when they do
surface, only the tips of their noses show. Seals have keen
eyesight and can easily spot someone walking on land, even if
he tries to conceal himself. They'll swim away and only return
when they think the person is gone. Who can blame them? If
I heard a strange noise, smelled a foreign scent, or saw an
unusual sight, I too would make tracks!

While Joe and I hunted, our wives worked very hard, too. They looked after the campsite, washed clothes, cooked meals (there was plenty of seal meat!), dried the cod we were also catching on that trip, and worked the sealskins, which we would take to the store in Rigolet to sell. By this time, the market for sealskins had opened up in Labrador, and we could get forty-two dollars for a ranger seal. Rigolet is quite far away from the hunting place where we spent a lot of time, at Sobok Bay, which is outside the cape. We had to travel along treacherous coastline through bad storms, high winds, and thick fog. But we needed to earn money one way or another. It really *doesn't* grow on trees!

One day, during the summer, while we were hunting near one of the islands outside the cape, low-flying plane with guns mounted on it passed overhead. We figured it was looking for something, but didn't spend a lot of time worrying about it. There were many seals in the water off that island, and we kept on with the hunt for several days, heading back and forth from our campsite, our little boat laden with seals.

We were out ranger hunting one day when we saw a low-flying plane that we later learned was looking for a submarine.

We were travelling south from Smokey with our cleaned and dried skins when we saw a big ship out in the deep water, and as we neared the island, two ships passed so close to us that we were rocking in their wake. One of the ships was full of artillery, and the crew members were waving at us. Then the vessels passed, and we continued to Rigolet to sell our skins. At the store, we talked with some other Inuit about the plane and the warships we'd seen. It turned out there had been a search going on; the U.S. military was out looking for a submarine. All boats out in the bay were supposed to be flying a flag, we were told.

We had been travelling in very dangerous waters; a submarine shell could have blown us apart, and we wouldn't even have known what hit us! I suddenly thought of the laundry we had hung out to dry on the mast. All those different colours, flying in the breeze—maybe that's why the ships had gotten so close to us; the crew couldn't figure out what flags we were flying! Some time later, when I was back in Nain for a visit, my stepfather told me that we had almost been bombed by a warship. The only thing that saved us, he said, was that Americans do not attack first; they only fight back when they have been hit.

Ranger hunting later in the spring, near Makkovik.

None of this stopped our hunt; there was one more trip to make before heading home. We were travelling west from the cape when we came across a group of rangers near the islands. It was very foggy, but we decided to stop at one of the islands because there were so many seals. We shot thirty rangers, camped long enough to dry the skins, and started back to Makkovik, skirting the outer islands. We were lucky to have enjoyed a very good summer of hunting.

Not long after that trip, I built a little house for me and
my wife. There was no lumber for sale at the store, so I had to
scrounge around for wood. I ended up having to go all the
way to Tassialuk, a full day's journey by boat from Makkovik.
Dina came along, and the two of us got some lumber that a
group of settlers had left behind. We had to pull it apart first,
because some of the pieces were nailed together and would
have been too big to fit in our boat.

But we got it home at last, and before too long we had our
own home. It was only twenty-by-twenty, but it was big
enough for the two of us. Besides, we didn't care how small it
was, as long as we had a house of our own.

Small Miracles

One evening after we had gone visiting, Dina and I met some people on the road who were going to church to receive communion. I suddenly got the strongest feeling that we were headed in the wrong direction—we were going home when we should have been going to church. When we got home, I said to Dina, "I wish we were going to communion services, like them."

Right then and there, my wife and I decided to start working towards confirmation in the church. We had both been baptized, but not confirmed.

So we talked to the minister about it, and he started giving us lessons. There were two other people in our confirmation class, a young woman named Amalia Semigak, and a young man, Eric Jararuse. We would meet at our house, sometimes taking instruction from the minister and sometimes from Julius Jararuse, Eric's uncle.

Dina, Amalia, and I made fast progress with our lessons, but Eric, who was blind, was having trouble and told me he wanted to quit. When the minister heard about this, he said that Eric had quit before, when he was taking lessons in Hebron. But the three of us decided to at least try to talk him out of it. At first he became very angry, saying he had made up his mind. But his anger waned when I said that because we had all started our lessons at the same time, we very much wanted to be confirmed together, as a united group. He agreed, and I undertook to help him with his work.

The bond between us—that we were both men—helped a lot in the learning-teaching process. It also seemed to work better for him to memorize his prayers by listening to me recite them, and I tried to be as patient as I could. Very quickly he began to pick things up, and soon we were all keeping pace, learning our prayers and preparing for our confirmation at Easter. At last the day arrived for us to give our recitation in church. We all got through without a single mistake. When we had finished, what joy! Then it was time for our first communion service. I was astonished at the sight of the communion wafer, a small, round disc no bigger than a quarter. How fragile it seemed, yet it embodied so much…

The winter after our confirmation, Dina, who was pregnant, went into premature labour and had to be rushed to the nursing station. I think it may have happened because she was working too hard, cleaning sealskins, but I'm not certain of that.

I wasn't home when she left the house, but my friend Andreas's wife came over later, when I had returned, to tell me that I had a son and that I was to go to the nursing station immediately. I hurried over and was met by a nurse and the minister, who told me that my new son would have to be baptized right away. When I got my first look at him, I understood why. He was a blue baby—his skin really did look blue, and he was so tiny and frail that I wondered how he could possibly survive.

My wife wanted him to have two names, but I thought he might not live if we gave him two names. I don't know why, exactly—maybe it was because I felt he was too small to bear the weight of more than one. When the minister asked for his name, I said, "Adam." That was my father's name.

Throughout the baptism, I prayed with all my might to God for my first-born son to live. I have never seen God. I only believe in him through reading his philosophy in books and through explanations by the minister. But I believe he heard my prayers. My son still lives, to this day.

We couldn't take Adam home right away. After the baptism, he had to stay inside an incubator because he was so small. But we could see him as much as we wanted. One time when I came to visit, the nurse told me that he could finally finish his bottle, which she showed me; it was no bigger than an eye-dropper!

As soon as he was strong enough, Adam was airlifted to the hospital in North West River for further medical attention. We were frightened for him again, not because he was worse but because the plane that arrived to pick him up got to Makkovik in the middle of a snowstorm, and we weren't even allowed to accompany him to North West River. It was a great relief when we got word that he had arrived safely.

Adam was still in the hospital when two friends proposed a caribou-hunting trip into the Makkovik hinterland in the early spring. But he was so much better that I decided I could go. We could use the meat, anyway. I was a bit surprised to be going caribou hunting, though; back in Nain, we would never be going so late.

The three of us went by dog team, travelling across several lakes south of Postville and along the southern shore of a big river before beginning the climb into the hinterland. The hills were very hard going, and I was thankful that the weather was turning clear, because it would have been difficult territory to negotiate in stormy or foggy conditions.

As we continued into the hinterland towards the hunting grounds, I could hardly believe that we were going into caribou-hunting territory. It was nothing like the countryside around Nain. The trees were so dense that it seemed unlikely that we would find a path through them, but one member of our party had been hunting in the area since childhood, and he knew the trail very well. I noticed that some of the trees had been marked with an axe and that there were well-worn paths in even the deepest parts of the woods.

When we reached the caribou-hunting grounds, there was just enough daylight for us to make camp. Again I was struck by the differences between hunting in the Makkovik area and the way we did things in Nain. The snow in the Makkovik hinterland wasn't that good for snow houses, because the dense forest kept the snow moist, and too soft to stick together and use as building blocks. So we always slept in a tent. I also noticed that Makkovik hunters even fed their dogs differently, cooking the seal meat with corn-meal in an oil drum that had been sawn in half. Back in Nain, our dogs always got their seal meat raw.

We were able to find caribou tracks without too much trouble, and shot quite a few caribou before making the long trip back to Makkovik, our sled heavy with meat. When I got home, my son was back from the hospital, and we celebrated with a feast—although Dina and I didn't give any caribou meat to our son just yet!

In the Makkovik hinterland, hunters set up tents to live in because the snow tends to stay too wet for building snow houses.

Lude's boat
got us safely
to the
hunting
ground in
Makkovik
where we
would go out
after ranger
seals.

Spring break-up was in full evidence, so the two of us began making preparations to go to the ranger-hunting grounds. Dina was pregnant again, and we had to make arrangements for Adam to stay with her grandparents, but we decided to make the trip together anyway. We couldn't take the chance of missing out on the hunt. Two relatives of mine, Tom and Lude, and their wives, travelled with us in Lude's boat.

The journey across the cape was much rougher this time, and I was sure we were all going to be blown overboard in the gale that came up during the crossing. But we were able to get around the cape safely and reach the hunting ground. We started in hunting as soon as we had pitched our tent. Our wives worked the skins as before.

Towards the end of the summer, just as we were getting ready to head home, Dina's baby was ready to be born and we couldn't get back to Makkovik in time for her to go to the nursing station. She gave birth in the tent, with the two women acting as midwives. I chopped wood all night to keep the tent warm for my wife and baby daughter.

When Dina and the baby were strong enough to travel, we returned to Makkovik, where we had her baptized in church, giving her the name Henrietta. Today, she lives in Saint John, New Brunswick, with her family.

It was a long night chopping wood to keep Dina warm while she gave birth.

Back in Nain

Dina and I and our new family spent the winter in Makkovik, and in the spring my mother and stepfather came to pick us up to go cod fishing in Nain for the summer. My wife and children stayed at my mother's house while I spent the summer at the fishing grounds where I had been going every since I was a young man. After the season was over, Dina and I decided to stay in Nain permanently. We didn't have our own house, so we moved in with my mother for a while. She would look after the children when Dina accompanied me on seal-hunting trips. That was another way Inuit families always helped each other through hard times.

The second summer I went cod fishing after we moved back to Nain, there were much fewer cod, so I decided to keep my eyes open for other work. A job came up the next spring on the government collector boat, the one that made the rounds of our northern communities, delivering supplies and picking up our catches.

At that time, a lot of Inuit fishermen were finding out, as I had, that the cod stocks were getting much lower. This was in the late 1960s and early 1970s, long before the latest disappearance of cod from our waters and those of Newfoundland. Inuit are not lazy fishermen, so they started going after char, sea trout, and salmon, often travelling long distances from Nain—to Nutak, Hebron, Saglek, and Nachvak. These were among the areas the collector boat visited when I was a crewman.

Sailing carries its risks. You have to know your sea route; you have to be careful when you are crossing a treacherous body of water. You have to remember where the shoals are, watch out for icebergs, and know the lay of the land. While the weather is fine, you study the land as you travel, making a mental chart of islands, bays, harbours, and landmarks. Then the fog will not impede your progress.

Sometimes, when you are journeying through dangerous waters, through storms and high waves, you can't help but be amazed that the boat stays afloat when it should surely sink or flounder. It's at times like these that a person doesn't play around. Silently, he prays to God that he may come to no harm.

Although it was spring when I started my stint on the collector boat, there was still a lot of ice and the going was rough and unpredictable. Once, when we were crossing the cape in the fog, we ran aground when gales and ice came into full play against us. We entered Napartok Bay for shelter and tried to leave again in the morning, but the harbour was packed solid with ice. I climbed the hill, and as far as the eye could see, there was heavy drift ice. We were trapped there for three weeks and nearly ran out of food. Finally the ice began to move out of the bay, and we were able to move out, keeping a constant watch on the boat's propeller. If the propeller had been broken or crushed, we would have been helpless.

Whenever we could, we tried to make our rounds quickly. The people in the fishing camps depended on us to deliver their food and other supplies, so we did our best. The other crewmen, like me, remembered what it was like to see the boat arrive without the supplies we had ordered from the store when we were out at the camps ourselves, cod fishing. We remembered having to make the trip back to Nain and try to get our orders filled. Just because we were now working on the boat, that didn't mean we could do anything about the store managers' continued refusal to send out everybody's supplies. We knew that some of the fishermen would have to make that trip at some point during the season, but at least we could try to get to their fishing places as quickly as possible and bring them what we could.

At fishing camp after fishing camp, we arrived to find anxious fishermen waiting for the boat. We would stop just long enough to unload the supplies, then set out again for the next camp, often sailing all night to make up time.

Even when the ice was gone, the job was not without its risks. There were often rough seas, gales, and bad fog. After one especially harrowing experience in the fog and storm off Nachvak Point, I was so scared that I wanted to quit. But I hung in till the end of the season, then surprised myself by agreeing to do the job again the following year. All this for $140.00 a month, on which I was supposed to support a large family—by the end of my second season on the freight boat, Dina and I had five children.

I wasn't the only one suffering because of a low salary. My fellow crewmen were in the same position, and all we could do was try to make ends meet as best we could.

Between that job, ranger hunting, and a few other odd jobs here and there, we were able to save enough to finally build a house in Nain. I bought two-by-fours and nails at the store, but when I asked for bigger boards, it was the same old story—they didn't have any and weren't going to order it. I bought some lumber from Inuit in Nain, then travelled north to Saglek to pick up more wood from an abandoned building there. It took a long time to get it all home on the "flat"— there were very high waves—and to carry it from the boat to the building site. But we were lucky enough to get twenty-four pieces of plywood, and it made a good house for us—still quite small, but solid.

My late wife and I built the house, while my mother baby-sat the children. The task is not hard when there is a goal in sight. We lived in that house for seven years, while my wife was still alive.

After my second summer on the collector boat, I was relieved that other jobs with the government were opening up, as employment became more varied in the 1970s. I had lost my taste for sailoring after all those experiences with the bad weather, and I don't know how long I could have continued doing it.

I don't remember all the different jobs I did, but none of them paid very much. One I do recall was unloading food, lumber, and other supplies from the collector boat when it came into Nain, loading the supplies onto a truck, and driving them up to the store. I earned $2.15 an hour for that job, often working far into the night without overtime. My co-workers were in the same situation. They had wives and children, too, and some of them earned even less than I did. But we didn't ever quit, any of us.

We're waiting for the freight boat to come in to Nain so we can start unloading the supplies and drive them over to the store.

Today-And Tomorrow

Some Inuit still try to maintain the old way of life. They go hunting, sealing, and fishing. They keep up the traditions of holidays and special days, and they participate in the choir or become chapel servants. People still try to help each other when they have problems; you still see Inuit in Nain getting together to help somebody build a house or lend a hand when somebody has lost a loved one.

But much has changed here since I was growing up, and all the efforts of people to maintain the old ways cannot erase these changes. Although people may go hunting and fishing, they cannot completely survive through these activities any longer, as far as I can see. Much of the fish and game, and even the seals, seem to be disappearing. Perhaps efforts to renew and replenish our environment will result in a return of our wildlife, but I am not sure this will happen in my lifetime. I can only hope our children will some day have the opportunity to experience nature as I did as a child—but without the hardship and heartbreak many of us lived through in those days.

The traditions of the community, too, are changing. When I was young, Inuit communities were organized by the elders, and they were respected. If there was a conflict between two people, the elders would meet with them and tell them how to resolve their difficulties. In those days, the church bell rang at nine o'clock to remind young people to go

How things have changed since I was a young boy!

home. If you were discovered outdoors after that time, a village elder would talk to you, then send you to your house. You never thought to disobey an elder.

Today there are so many government agencies—the RCMP, the Labrador Inuit Association, the Department of Social Services—that it is difficult to know who to turn to. And the community is so much bigger that it is not always possible for the spirit of co-operation among people to flourish as it once did. Jobs are more scarce than ever, and people are no longer able to live as hunters. Young people drink alcohol, stay out late, and get into trouble. There is little work for them and they can easily lose hope.

I still went out hunting and fishing once in a while, but it's as I said before: there weren't enough animals or fish for me to be able to earn a living that way. And seeing all the snowmobiles out in the wilderness was another sad reminder of how much things had changed.

There wasn't very much other work I could do, so I went to live in government housing after my money ran out, and I got some through support from the government. That wasn't how I wanted to live, though.

I suppose all these things are the sum total of why I started drinking and doing things that were wrong. I kept ending up in jail because alcohol consumed and controlled my mind, and I would go out and get into trouble. Last time I was in jail for being drunk in public, and for what they call "making verbal threats," which means that I was threatening to hit someone. Also, I had violated my probation just by

Sometimes, there seem to be so many agencies that you don't know which one to turn to.

This picture is very grey and sad because it represents the loss of freedom when a person has to go to jail.

being drunk out in public in the first place.

I am describing these events as a way of starting to take control over them. Sometimes just admitting what has gone wrong can help you begin to make it right again. At the Alcoholics Anonymous meetings I have attended, we always begin by giving our name and saying, "I am an alcoholic." This way, we do not so readily run away from the problem by going right back to the bottle again, as if it were a solution. Instead, we try to face our problems and look for ways to make our lives better.

For me, the people at AA, along with my probation officer and my friends, have done a lot to help. I am also encouraged by some of the developments I see happening in Nain to respond to the difficulties people are having here. There are more educational opportunities for young people to develop skills that will help them get good jobs. There are retraining programs to help older people adjust to the changes in the job market. And there are groups in which we can all talk about the future of our community.

One committee whose meetings I have attended is trying very hard to improve things by putting more emphasis on taking control of our own affairs. One example is that we are trying to have the government store become a co-operative run by Inuit. We have also expressed a desire to have more of a say in other aspects of government, such as policing and the justice system.

For myself, something else has come into my life, something that makes me feel the way I did as a young boy, when the land began to awaken with new life in the spring. That something is these words and these drawings.

Like going on a hunting trip, or building a house, or supporting a family, or learning to live with loss and change, telling stories and creating images about the experiences of your life can be rough going at first. You sometimes have to go through quite a struggle before the memories and thoughts in your mind start to come out on the page the way they happened.

But you don't ever quit when something is important to you. That's something I learned by growing up in a community where people depended on each other for their very survival. Of course, writing a book might seem a little different from that. Some people might not think it has anything to do with anyone's survival. But in a way, it does.

Remembering the events and experiences of my life has given me new hope for my own future. In writing about them and drawing pictures of them, I began to realize just how unique and valuable our Inuit tradition is. And I began to feel that my own life has a new meaning because I am a part of that tradition.

Now that the book is finished, I hope those who hear these stories and see these pictures will also discover the value of the heritage the Inuit have to offer.

If we feel we are of value, we have a reason to survive.